THE HAPPY BIRTHDAY MYSTERY

Joan Lowery Nixon

Pictures by Jim Cummins

ALBERT WHITMAN & COMPANY, CHICAGO

J
N

Library of Congress Cataloging in Publication Data

Nixon, Joan Lowery.
    The happy birthday mystery.

    (First read-alone mysteries)
    SUMMARY: Two amateur sleuths track down Mrs.
Pickett's missing birthday cake.
    [1. Mystery and detective stories. 2. Birthdays
—Fiction] I. Cummins, James. II. Title.
PZ7.N65Hap   [E]   79-18362
ISBN 0-8075-3150-2

With love to Mary Lou Bodnar,
in remembrance of the many birthdays
we have enjoyed together.

Mike held the cardboard box carefully. "Knock on Mrs. Pickett's door," he told Susan.

"I hope she likes angel food," Susan said.

"Sh-shh," Mike whispered. "This cake is supposed to be a birthday surprise. What good is a surprise if it isn't a secret?"

Just then Mrs. Pickett opened the door. "A surprise that isn't a secret?" she said. "You've got another spotted dinosaur riddle! Let's see . . . how do you get a spotted dinosaur to keep a secret?"

"No, Mrs. Pickett," Susan said. "This isn't a riddle."

"Then I'll ask *you* a riddle," Mrs. Pickett said. "What would you do if a spotted dinosaur sat in front of you at the movies?"

"I don't know," Mike said.

"Miss most of the movie!" Mrs. Pickett clapped her hands.

"That's a good joke, Mrs. Pickett," Mike said. "We're going for a walk in the park. Would you like to come with us?"

"I'd love to," Mrs. Pickett said. She looked at the box. "Why don't you leave that box here while we're gone?"

"Oh, no," Mike said. "There's something inside that we'll need."

Mike, Susan, and Mrs. Pickett headed for
the park. When they got there, they saw
some people near the duck pond.

Two girls on roller skates hurried to join
the group. A boy wearing a baseball cap
with a star on it rode past them on his
bike.

10

In front of the people Susan saw a boy
waving a string of silk scarves. He had
on a tall, black hat.

"It's a magician!" she said. "Come on!"

They hurried to see the magician. Susan
put the cake box on an empty bench.

The magician was wearing a false mustache and a big coat. He waved his hands over his head and pulled a huge bunch of paper flowers out of the air.

"Wonderful!" Mrs. Pickett shouted.

The magician gave Mrs. Pickett a deep bow. His hat fell off. Everyone laughed.

"Show us more tricks," Mrs. Pickett said.

The magician put his hat on the ground. He pulled a rabbit out of the hat. Then he made the rabbit disappear.

He pulled coins out of his fingers and cards out of the air. Then the rabbit jumped out of his coat pocket.

"Would you like me to hold your rabbit?"
Mrs. Pickett asked.

"Yes," said the magician. "You can be my
assistant."

Mrs. Pickett stroked the rabbit. "I love
animals," she said to the boy wearing the
star baseball cap.

"You do?" the boy said.

The magician did some more tricks. "Do you think it's really magic?" Mrs. Pickett asked the boy with the cap. But the boy was gone.

At last the magician said, "That's all. The show is over. Thank you very much." He took the rabbit from Mrs. Pickett. Then he gave another bow. This time he held onto his hat.

Everyone clapped. Susan saw that the boy wearing the baseball cap was back again. He was smiling and clapping, too.

Susan and Mike and Mrs. Pickett went to the bench where Susan had set the cake box. Susan picked up the box. "Follow me to the picnic tables," she said.

"We have a surprise for you in this box," Mike said. "Because it's your birthday!"

"I'm so excited!" Mrs. Pickett said. "I didn't think anyone would remember my birthday."

She opened the box and looked inside.
"Oh, my!" she said. "What a lovely
birthday present. Something I've always
wanted!"

She reached inside the box and pulled out
a small, black kitten.

Susan and Mike stared at the kitten.
"What happened to the cake?" Susan
gasped.

"A birthday cake can't turn into a kitten,"
Mike said.

"Not unless it's magic," Susan said.

"But birthdays have something to do with magic," Mrs. Pickett said. "When you blow out the candles on a birthday cake, you're trying to work magic. You want your wish to come true."

Susan shrugged. "That magician must have changed the cake into a kitten."

"He couldn't." Mike looked puzzled.

Suddenly Susan saw someone watching them. It was the boy wearing the star baseball cap.

"That's a nice kitten," the boy said to Mrs. Pickett.

"He's my birthday present," Mrs. Pickett said. She snuggled the kitten under her chin. "Isn't he lovely?"

"Can you keep pets where you live?" the boy asked.

"Oh, yes," Mrs. Pickett said.

"That's good," the boy said. "Well, happy birthday." He rode away on his bike.

"We have to find that magician," Susan
said. "We have to find out what he did
with our cake."

She looked inside the box. There was
nothing there but a ragged shirt that had
been a bed for the kitten.

"Wait a minute," Mike said. "Look at the
box. We put our cake in a tomato soup
box. But this box is for canned peas!"

"That's it!" Susan said. "Someone switched boxes."

"Or maybe the kitten ate the cake!" Mrs. Pickett laughed.

Mike said, "Mrs. Pickett, we think someone took the box with your cake in it and left the box with the kitten. We're going back to the bench. We have to look for clues."

"I'll come, too," Mrs. Pickett said. "Maybe the kitten and I can help."

Susan, Mike, and Mrs. Pickett hurried back to the duck pond. They saw a boy with a cardboard grocery box.

"Have you got our cake in your box?" Susan shouted to the boy.

"No," he said. "I've got my magician's coat and hat in here."

"Oh, I'm sorry," Susan said. "I didn't know you were the magician without your hat and mustache."

Mike asked, "Did you see anyone at the show with a cardboard box?"

The magician looked at Susan. "She had
one."

"Anyone else?" Mike asked.

"Yes," the magician said. "I saw someone
with another box, but when I looked
again, he was gone. Now you see him,
now you don't. Maybe he'll show up
again. Maybe he's hiding right now."

"That makes me think of another spotted
dinosaur riddle," Mrs. Pickett said. "How
do you know a spotted dinosaur has been
hiding in your refrigerator?"

"You got me," said the magician.

"You can see his footprints in the butter!"
Mrs. Pickett laughed so hard she almost
dropped the kitten.

"This is serious, Mrs. Pickett," said Susan. "I'm thinking about someone at the magic show who disappeared and then came back. Someone who's been very interested in Mrs. Pickett and the kitten."

Mike thought a minute. "I think I know who you mean," he said. "Let's look in the box again to see if there's any other clue."

Susan held up the T-shirt that had been the kitten's bed. The shirt had a faded star on the front. Susan and Mike laughed.

Mike whispered, "Maybe the magician is
right. Maybe the mystery person is hiding
near us right now. I'm going to try a
trick."

In a loud voice Mike said, "It's too bad
you can't keep the kitten, Mrs. Pickett."

The boy with the star baseball cap
appeared from behind some bushes.

He looked at Mrs. Pickett. "I thought you
liked the kitten," he said. "I thought you
were going to take care of him."

"She does like the kitten," Susan said.
"And she's going to keep him. But we
want you to give us back our cake."

The boy looked surprised. "Here's your
cake. I was going to give it back later.
We're moving and I had to find a good
home for my kitten."

Susan said, "When the magician told us,
'Now you see him, now you don't,' I
remembered that you left the magic show
and came back. You had just enough time
to switch boxes."

30

"You were awfully interested in Mrs. Pickett's kitten," said Mike. "And the star on the T-shirt in the box is just like the star on your hat."

"I'd like some of that cake now," Mrs. Pickett said. "I'm sure there will be enough for all of us—even H.B."

"Are you H.B.?" the boy asked Mike.

"He's Mike," Susan said. "And I'm Susan. H.B. must be the kitten's new name. And any good detective would know what H.B. stands for."

"Happy birthday!" Mike said.

"Thank you," Mrs. Pickett said. "It's been a very happy birthday, indeed!"